Mel Bay Presents

The new sound of FUNK BASS

by Josquin des Pres

☐ CD Tracks ◯ Play Along Tracks

Track		Track		Track	
[1]	Example 1	[31]	Example 16	[61]	Example 31
(2)	Example 1	(32)	Example 16	(62)	Example 31
[3]	Example 2	[33]	Example 17	[63]	Example 32
(4)	Example 2	(34)	Example 17	(64)	Example 32
[5]	Example 3	[35]	Example 18	[65]	Example 33
(6)	Example 3	(36)	Example 18	(66)	Example 33
[7]	Example 4	[37]	Example 19	[67]	Example 34
(8)	Example 4	(38)	Example 19	(68)	Example 34
[9]	Example 5	[39]	Example 20	[69]	Example 35
(10)	Example 5	(40)	Example 20	(70)	Example 35
[11]	Example 6	[41]	Example 21	[71]	Example 36
(12)	Example 6	(42)	Example 21	(72)	Example 36
[13]	Example 7	[43]	Example 22	[73]	Example 37
(14)	Example 7	(44)	Example 22	(74)	Example 37
[15]	Example 8	[45]	Example 23	[75]	Example 38
(16)	Example 8	(46)	Example 23	(76)	Example 38
[17]	Example 9	[47]	Example 24	[77]	Example 39
(18)	Example 9	(48)	Example 24	(78)	Example 39
[19]	Example 10	[49]	Example 25	[79]	Example 40
(20)	Example 10	(50)	Example 25	(80)	Example 40
[21]	Example 11	[51]	Example 26	[81]	Example 41
(22)	Example 11	(52)	Example 26	(82)	Example 41
[23]	Example 12	[53]	Example 27	[83]	Example 42
(24)	Example 12	(54)	Example 27	(84)	Example 42
[25]	Example 13	[55]	Example 28	[85]	Example 43
(26)	Example 13	(56)	Example 28	(86)	Example 43
[27]	Example 14	[57]	Example 29	[87]	Example 44
(28)	Example 14	(58)	Example 29	(88)	Example 44
[29]	Example 15	[59]	Example 30	[89]	Example 45
(30)	Example 15	(60)	Example 30	(90)	Example 45

1 2 3 4 5 6 7 8 9 0

Visit us on the Web at www.melbay.com — E-mail us at email@melbay.com

Introduction

Over the past decade, funk music has branched into a diversity of styles. Spawned by Hip Hop, Acid Jazz and Neo-Soul the new sound of funk combines new millennium grooves with classic funk and R&B roots.

When it comes to funk, no instrument has contributed more than the electric bass and no decades are more important to funk bass than the 60's and 70's. That's why most current Hip Hop, R&B, Neo Soul and Acid Jazz players turn to the early days of funk for more traditional sources of inspiration.

The New Sound Of Funk Bass provides over 90 bass lines played over 45 fully produced tracks reminiscent of old school funk combined with new groove R&B. Each example is followed by a play along version without the bass. These tracks will not only help you learn and perform the dozens of recorded and transcribed bass lines, but will also serve as a springboard to help you create your own original bass grooves.

About the Author

Session bass player, author, producer and songwriter **Josquin des Pres** began his career in France in the mid 1970's, when he obtained his first record deal signing his fusion band with RCA Records. He has since shared credits with some of the biggest names in the music industry: **Jeff Porcaro, Alex Acuna, Vinny Colaiuta, Jerry Donahue, Billy Sheehan, Nick D'Virgilio, Bunny Brunel, Steve Lukather, David Garibaldi, Jerry Goodman, Jimmy Crespo, Scott Gorham, Steve Lukather, Didier Lockwood** and many others...

In addition to his career as a bass player Josquin des Pres has authored 14 best selling bass instruction books, 2 guitar instruction books and released ***Old School Funk Bass,*** distributed by Big Fish Audio, a CD-ROM of over 500 of his funkiest bass lines in audio and Acid Loop formats.

Josquin has also taken an interest in matters pertaining to the music industry and the success of musicians within the business. This has lead to the writing of two self-help titles: ***Creative Careers In Music*** and ***Reality Check.***

As a producer and songwriter, Josquin has worked on hundreds of recordings and has had numerous songs covered by international artists. He is one of the very few to collaborate on several songs with Elton John's legendary lyricist **Bernie Taupin.**

CD Credits and Acknowledgements

Bass: **Josquin des Pres**
Drums: **Michael Evans**
Guitar: **Bernard Torelli & David Stark**
Keyboards: **Carl Evans, Bernard Torelli & Scott Gorham**
Saxophone & Flute: **Chris Klich**
Recorded, edited, mixed and mastered at Track Star Studios La Mesa, California 91941 USA
Recording and mixing engineer: **Bernard Torelli**
ProTools editing & mastering **Fabien Renoult**
Assistant engineer: **Sean Morrissey**
Cover art: **Fabien Renoult**
Notation proofing: **Phil Dolganov**

Josquin des Pres uses Carvin and Vigier basses, La Bella Strings, MOTU recording software and hardware, Nomad Factory Plug–Ins, Tannoy Speakers.

Special Thanks to: Nam Chi Vu, Tristan des Pres, Phil Dolganov, Fabien Renoult, Bernie Torelli, Sean Morrissey, Mark Keisel, Richard Cocco, Bob Archigian, Irv Weisman and all the great musicians who played on the audio CD.

Example 1

CD Track Number 1
Play Along Track #2

Example 2

CD Track Number 3
Play Along Track #4

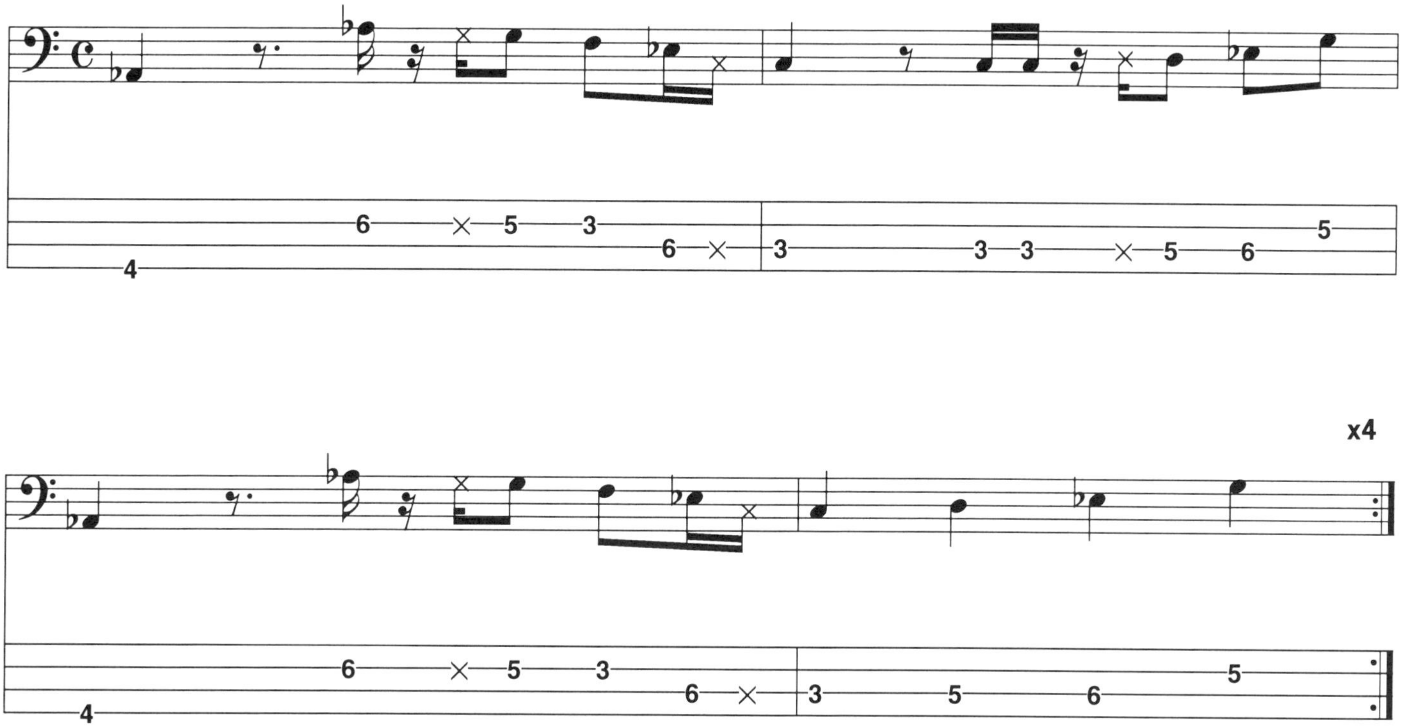

Example 3

CD Track Number 5
Play Along Track #6

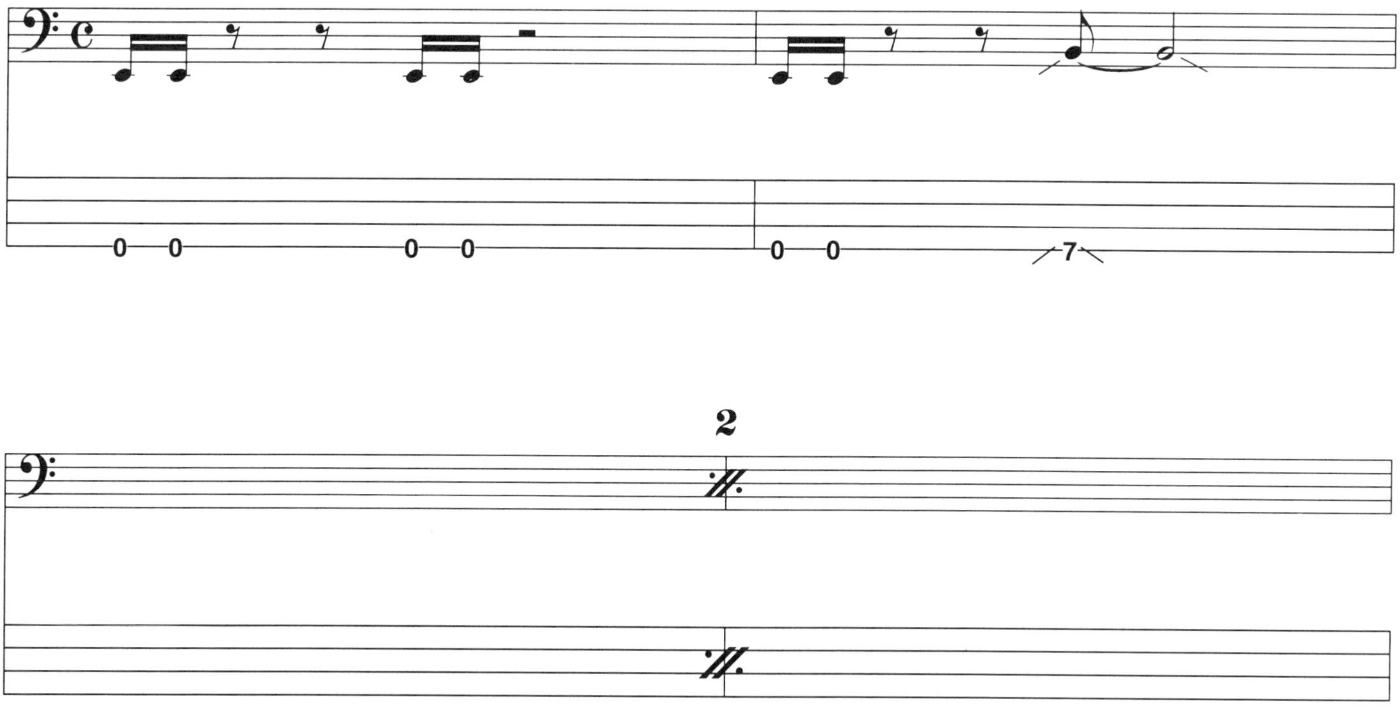

Example 4

CD Track Number 7

Play Along Track #8

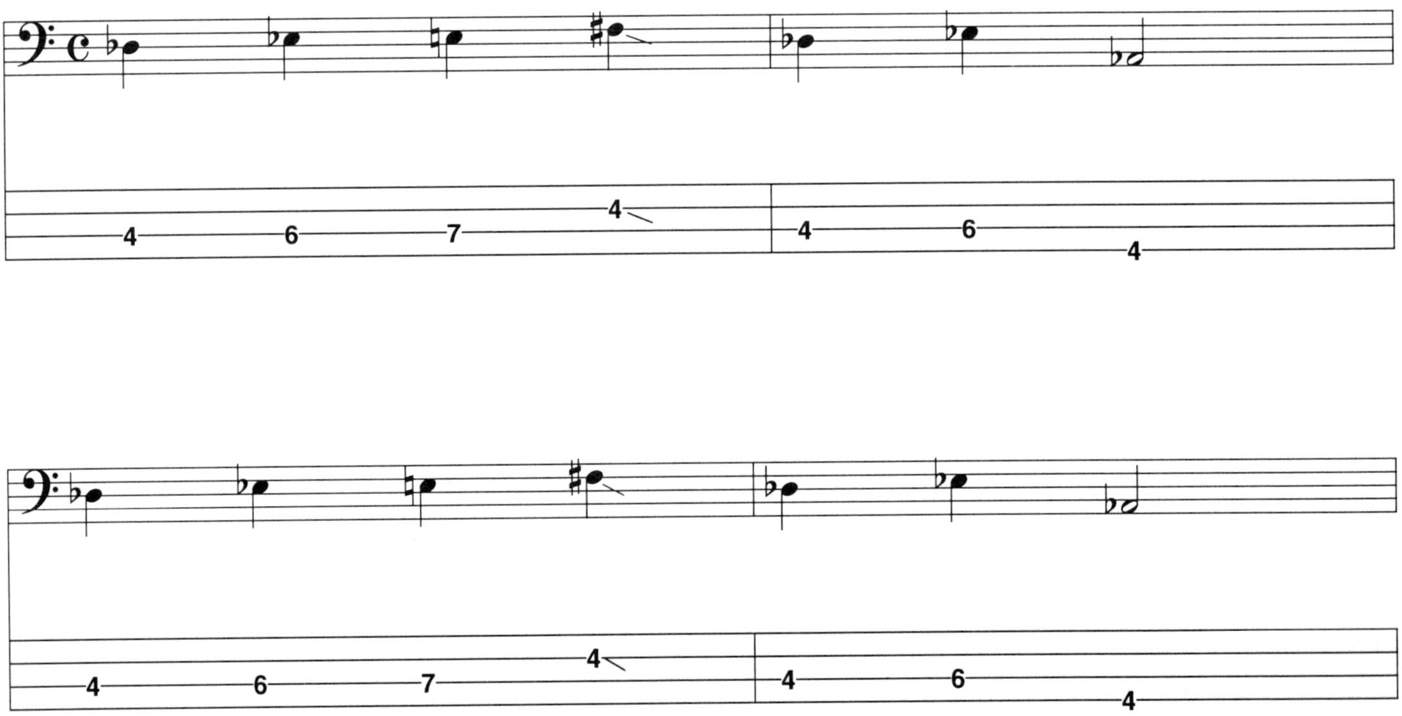

2
2

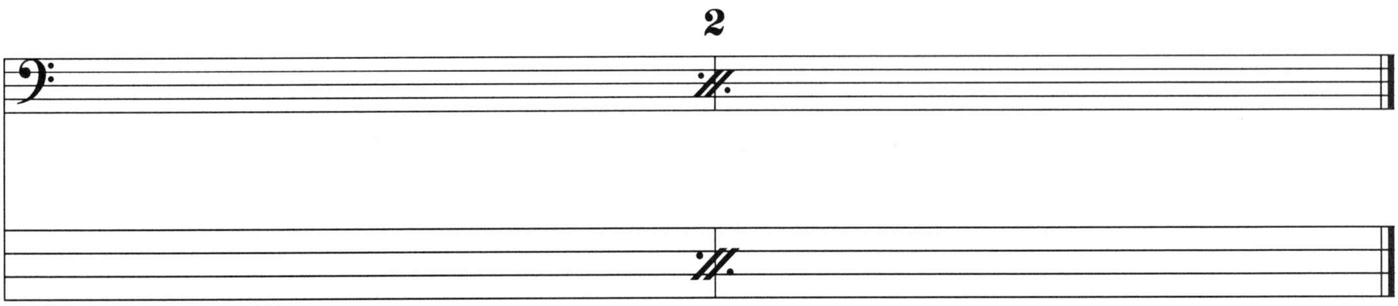

Example 5

CD Track Number 9

Play Along Track #10

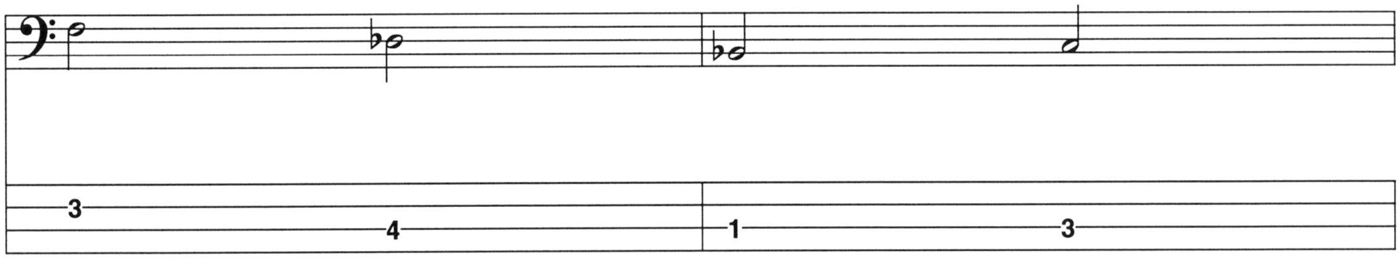

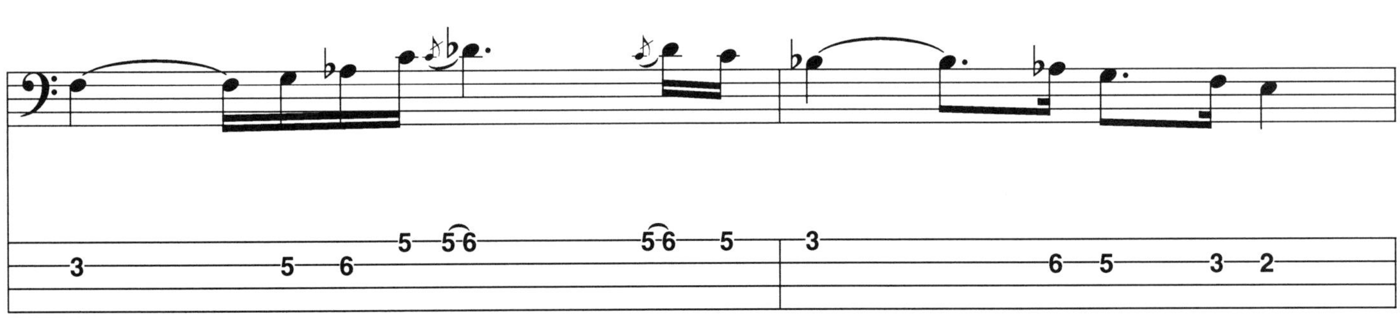

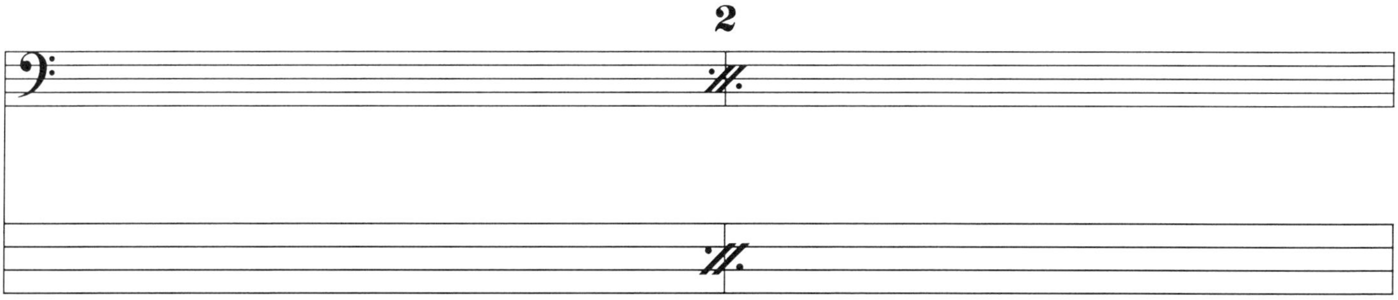

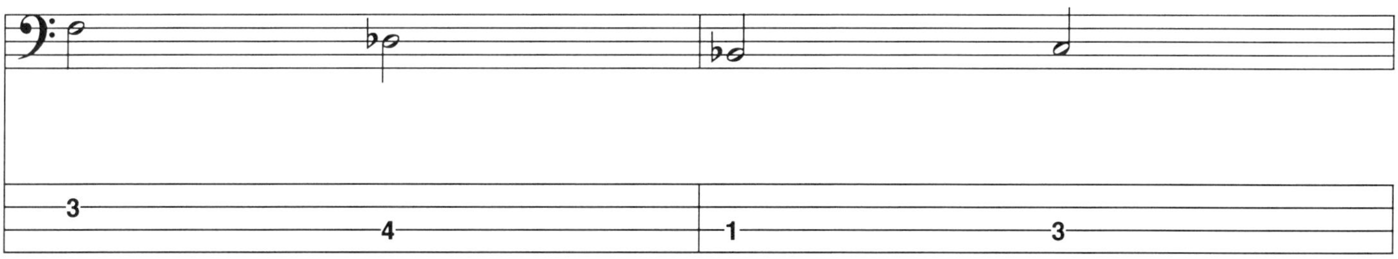

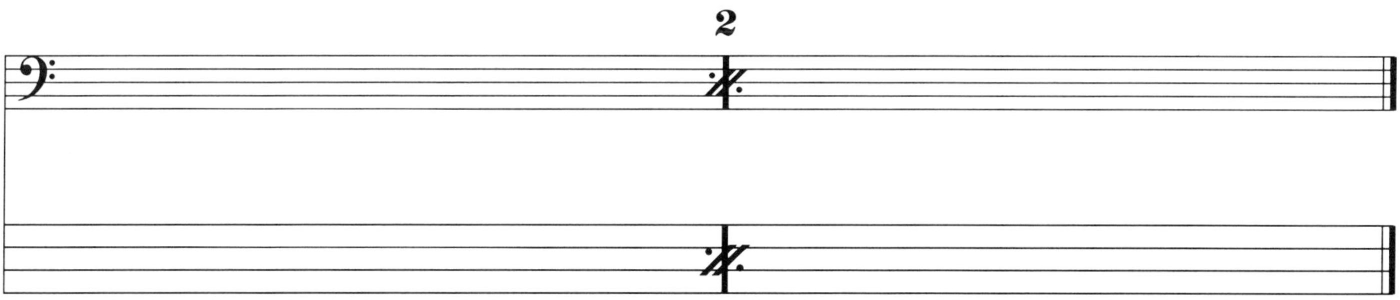

Example 6

CD Track Number 11

Play Along Track #12

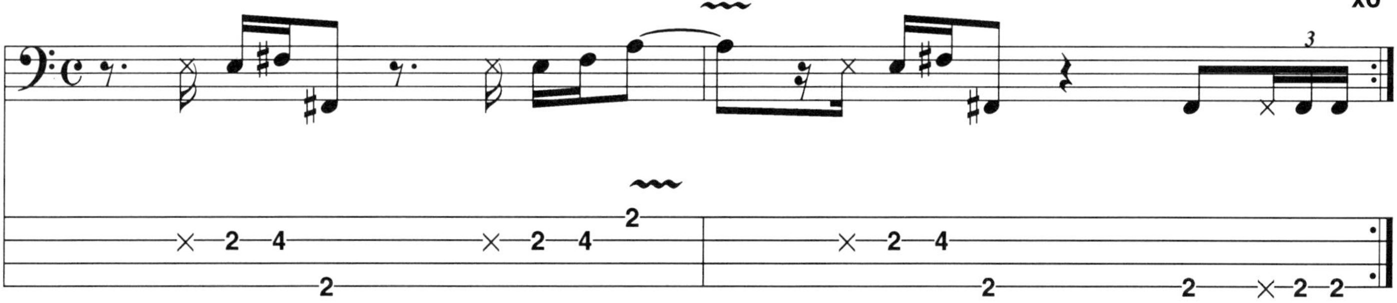

Example 7

CD Track Number 13
Play Along Track #14

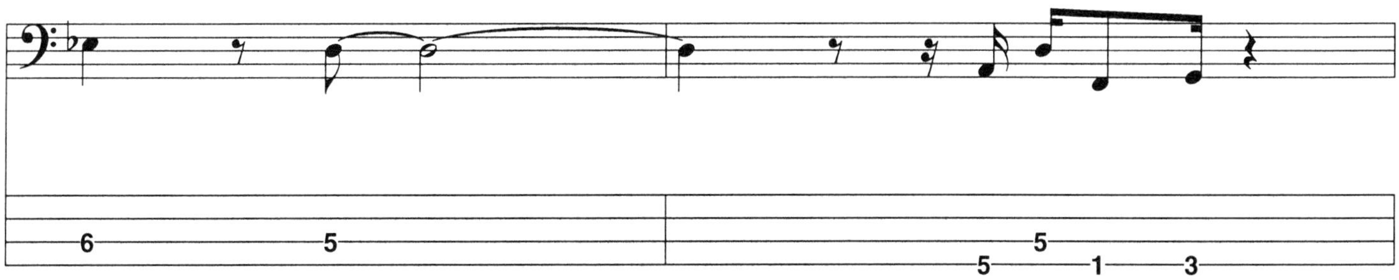

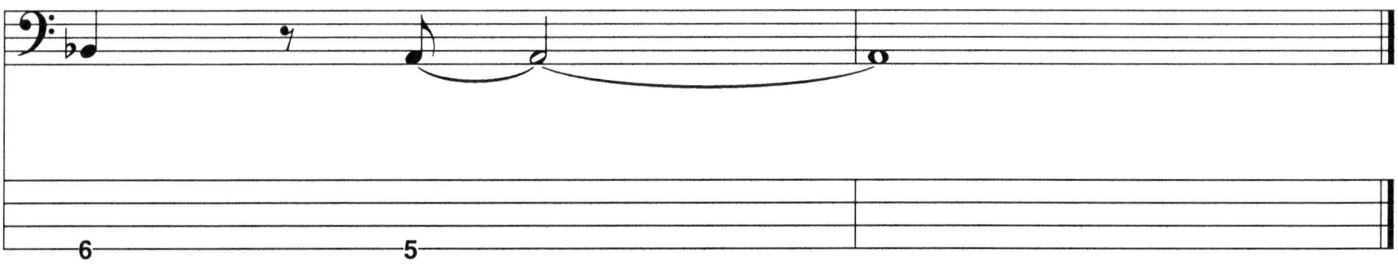

Example 8

CD Track Number 15
Play Along Track #16

x6

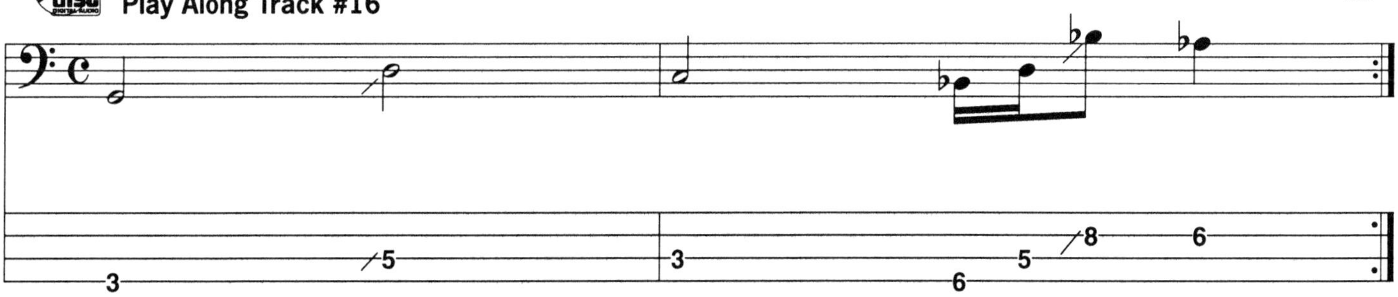

Example 9

CD Track Number 17
Play Along Track #18

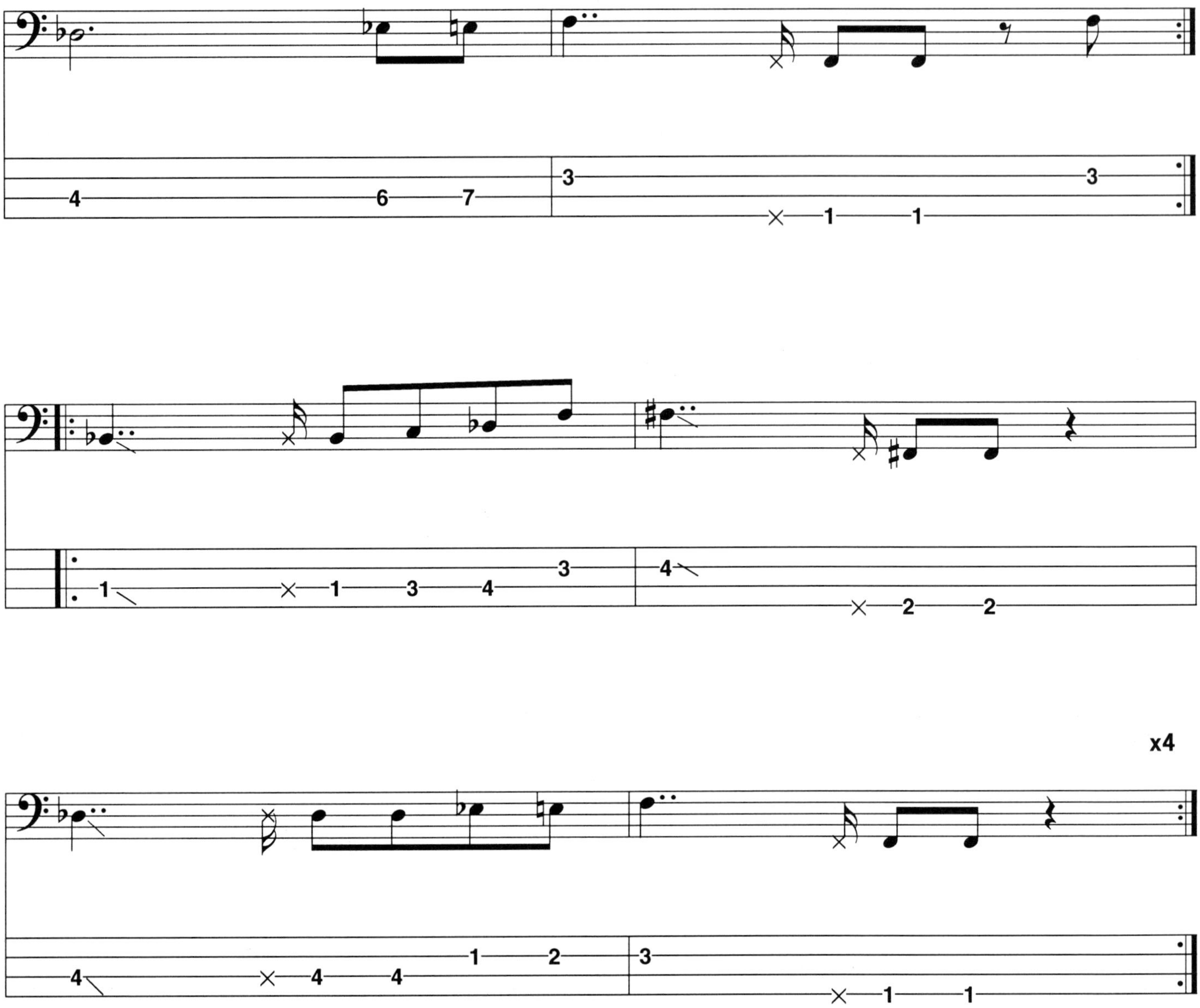
x4

Example 10

CD Track Number 19
Play Along Track #20

Example 11

CD Track Number 21

Play Along Track #22

Swing Feel

Example 12

CD Track Number 23
Play Along Track #24

Example 13

CD Track Number 25
Play Along Track #26

Example 14

CD Track Number 27
Play Along Track #28

Swing Feel

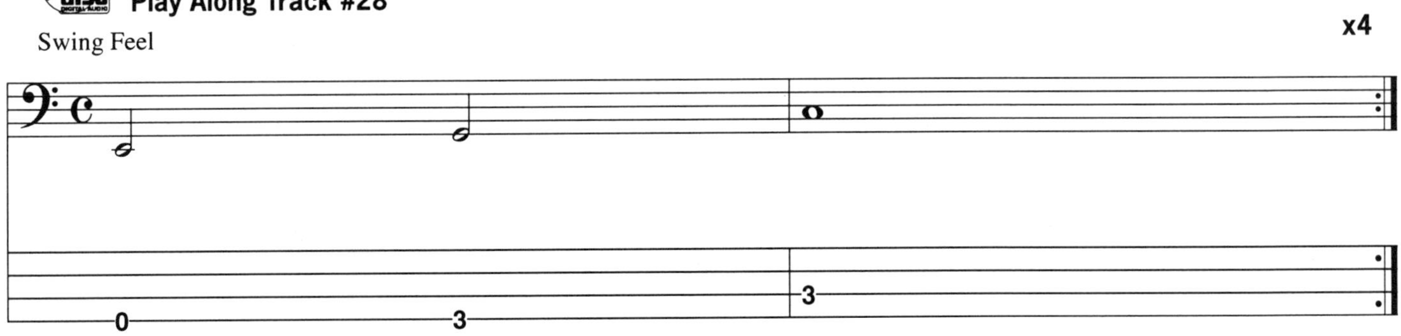

Example 15

CD Track Number 29

Play Along Track #30

Example 16

CD Track Number 31
Play Along Track #32

Swing Feel

Example 17

CD Track Number 33
Play Along Track #34

Example 18

CD Track Number 35
Play Along Track #36

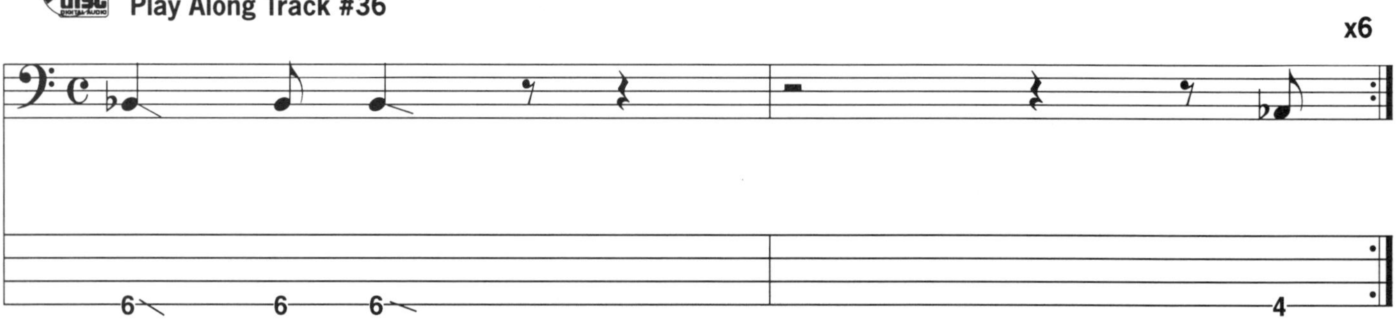

Example 19

CD Track Number 37
Play Along Track #38

Example 20

CD Track Number 39
Play Along Track #40

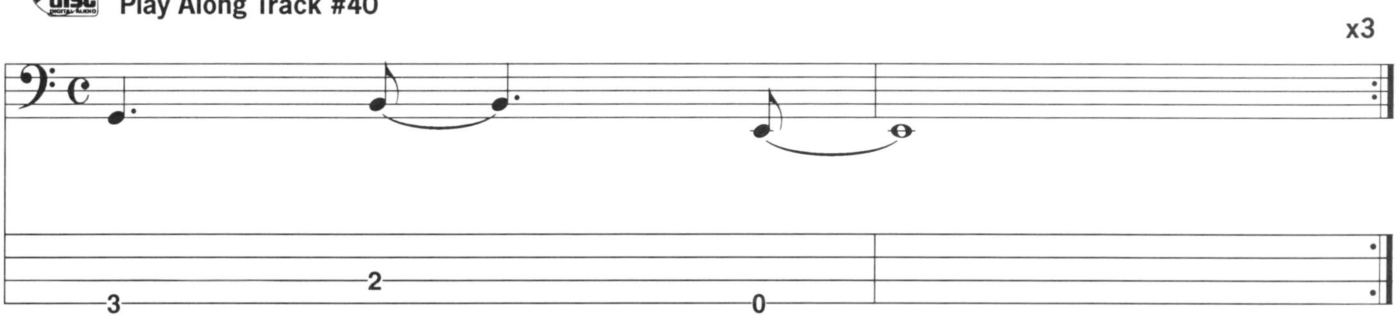

Example 21

CD Track Number 41
Play Along Track #42

Example 22

CD Track Number 43
Play Along Track #44

Example 23

CD Track Number 45
Play Along Track #46

Swing Feel

Example 24

CD Track Number 47
Play Along Track #48

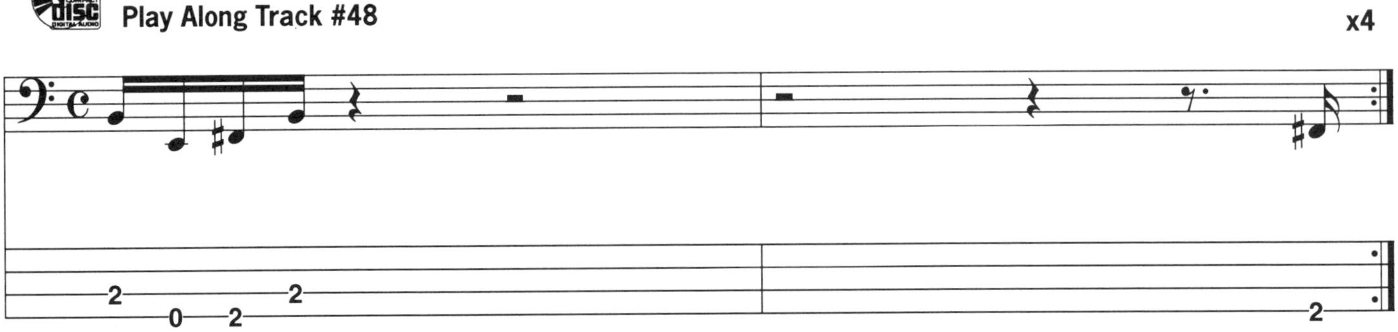

Example 25

CD Track Number 49
Play Along Track #50

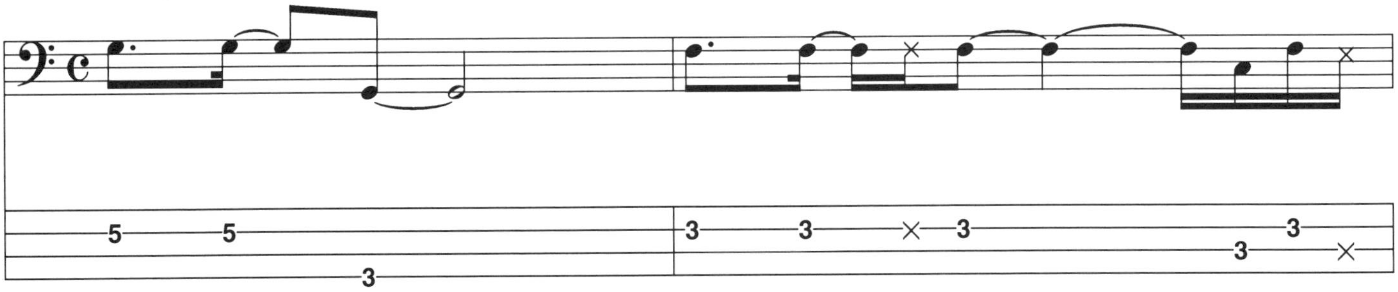

Example 26

CD Track Number 51

Play Along Track #52

Example 27

CD Track Number 53

Play Along Track #54

Swing Feel

x8

Example 28

CD Track Number 55

Play Along Track #56

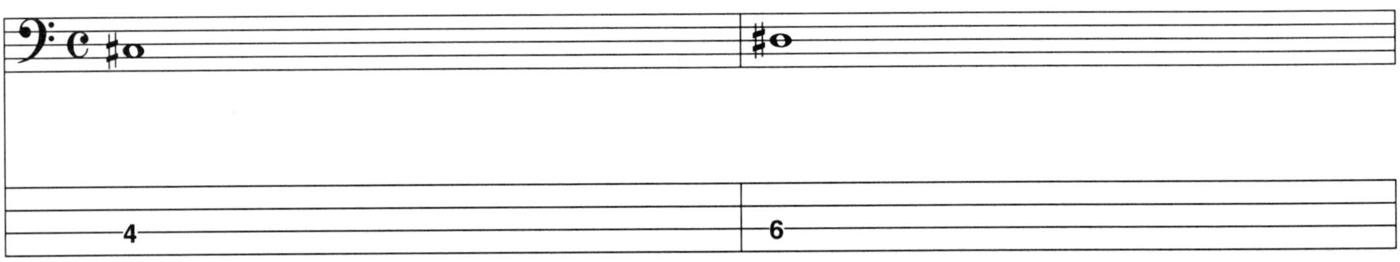

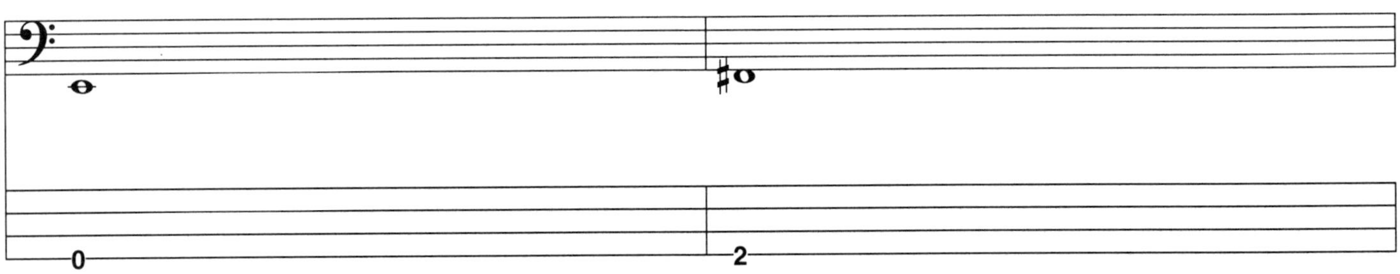

Example 29

CD Track Number 57

Play Along Track #58

x4

x4

Example 30

CD Track Number 59

Play Along Track #60

x4

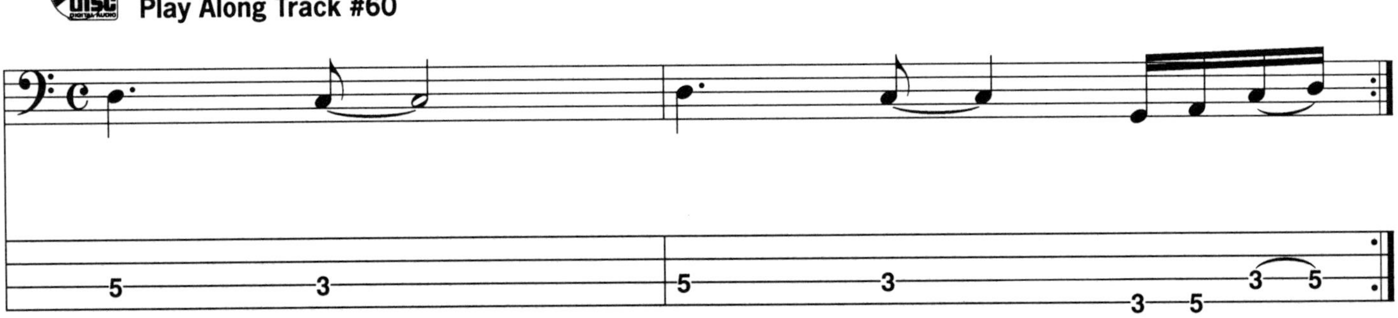

Example 31

CD Track Number 61
Play Along Track #62

x4

Example 32

CD Track Number 63
Play Along Track #64

x6

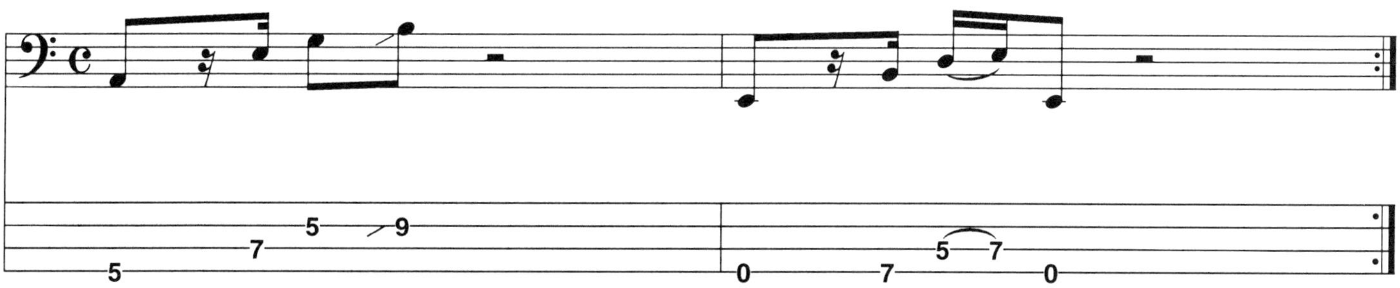

Example 33

CD Track Number 65

Play Along Track #66

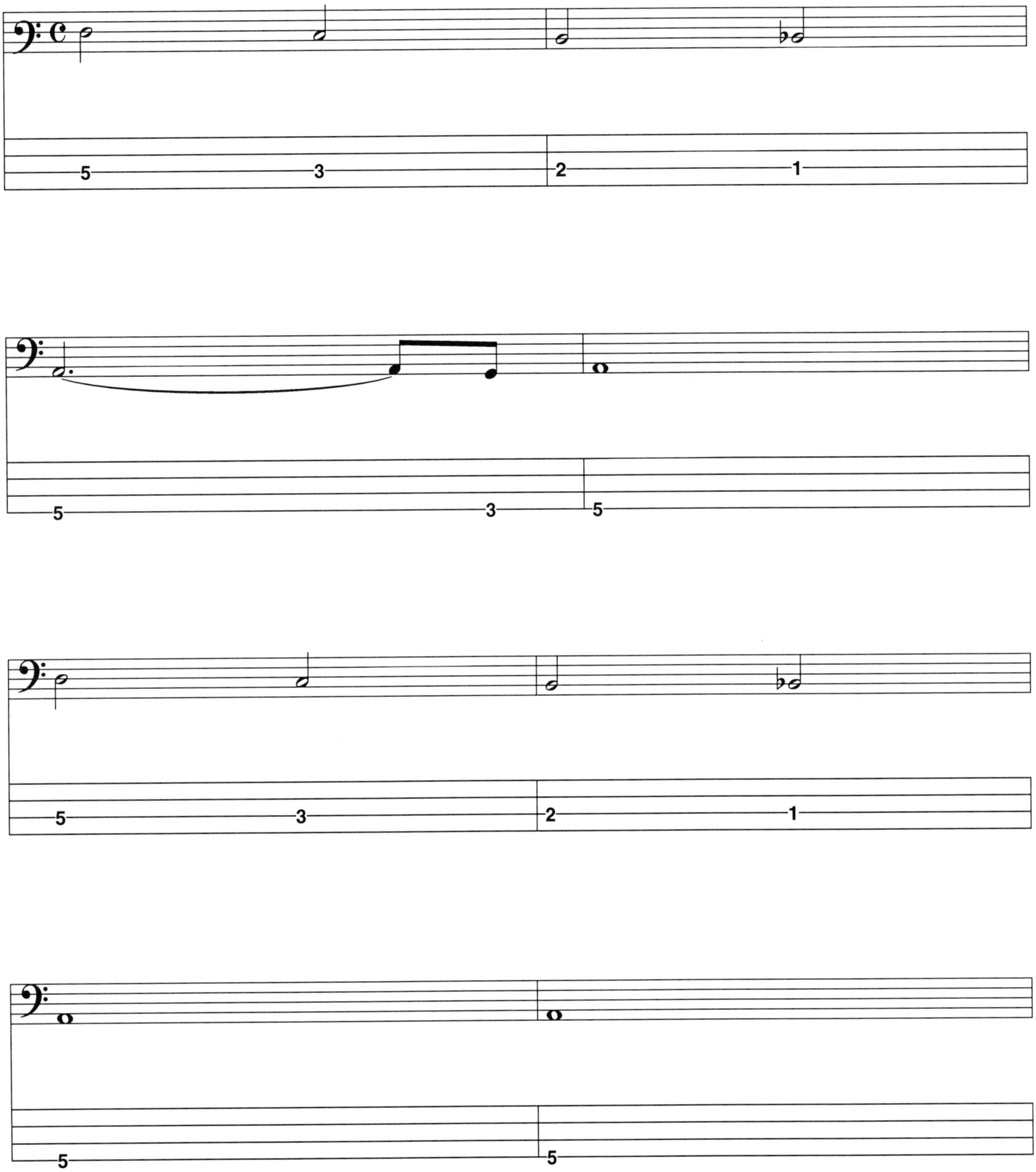

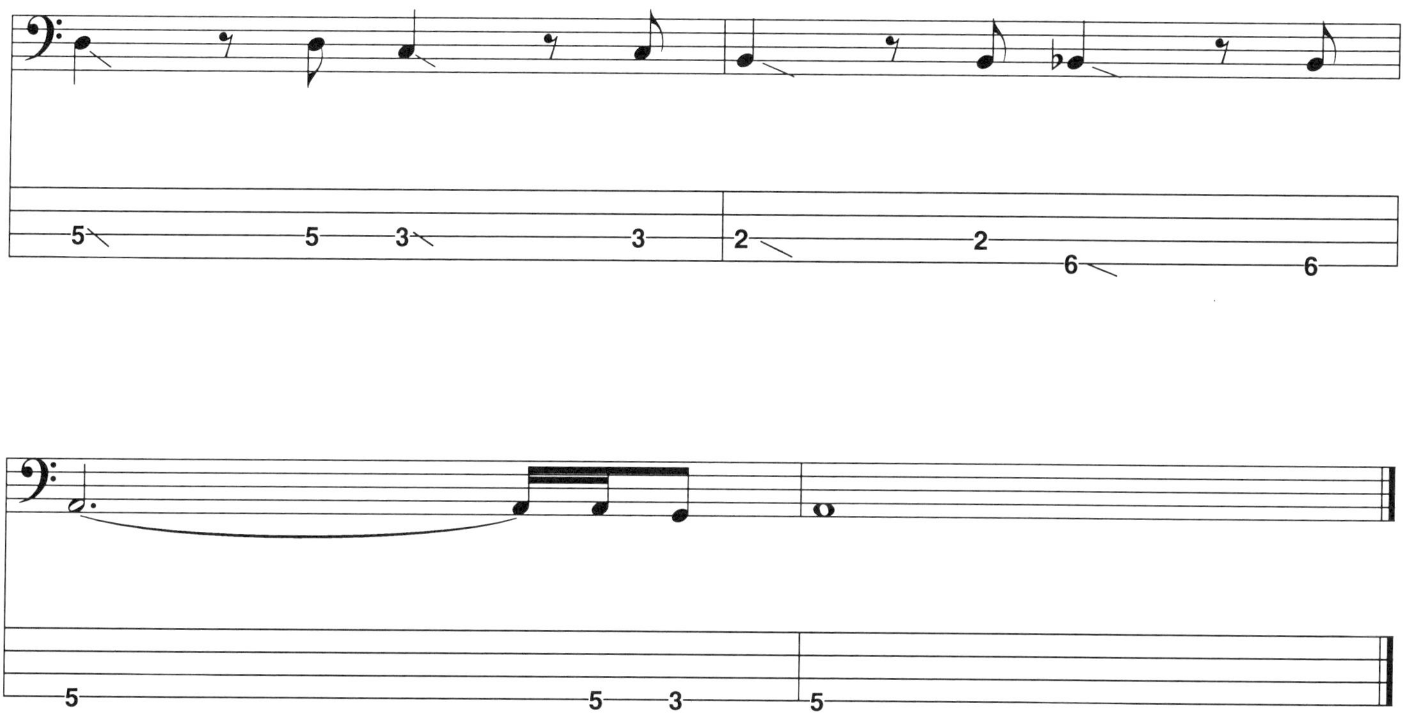

Example 34

CD Track Number 67

Play Along Track #68

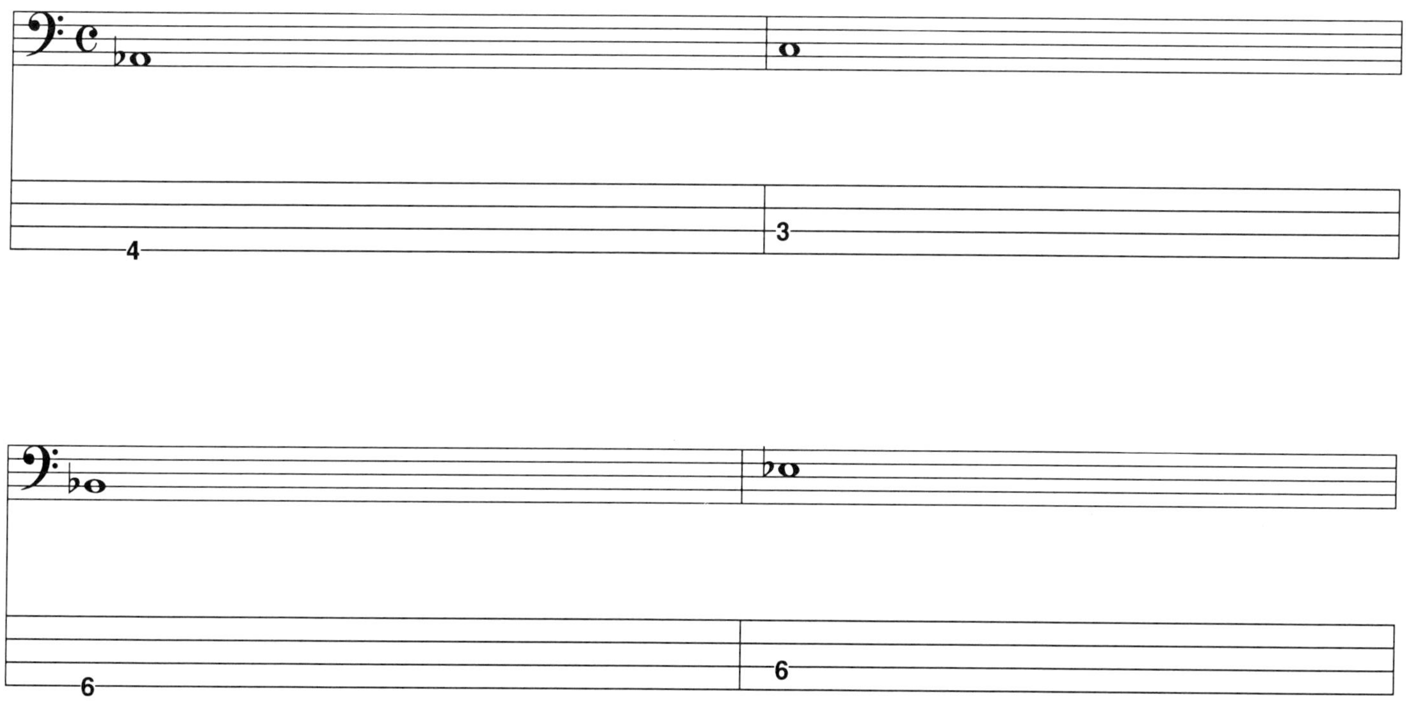

x3

Example 35

CD Track Number 69
Play Along Track #70

Example 36

CD Track Number 71
Play Along Track #72

Example 37

CD Track Number 73
Play Along Track #74

Example 38

CD Track Number 75

Play Along Track #76

Example 39

CD Track Number 77
Play Along Track #78

Example 40

CD Track Number 79
Play Along Track #80

x10

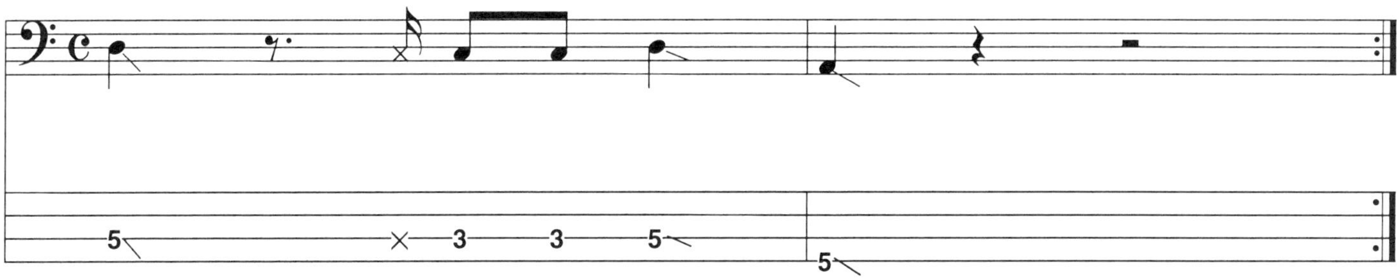

Example 41

CD Track Number 81
Play Along Track #82

Example 42

CD Track Number 83

Play Along Track #84

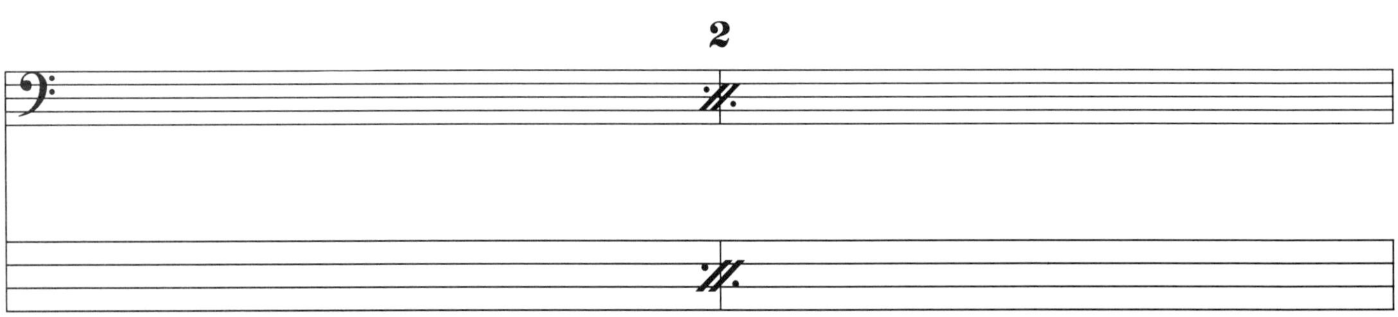

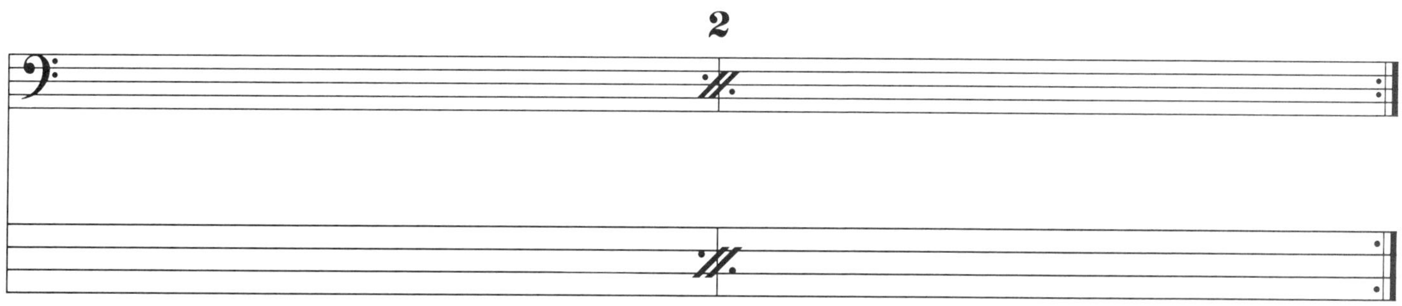

Example 43

CD Track Number 85
Play Along Track #86

Example 44

CD Track Number 87
Play Along Track #88

Example 45

CD Track Number 89

Play Along Track #90